Lineberger Memorial Library

Lutheran Theological Southern Seminary   Columbia, S. C.

The Little Hippos' Adventure

Rabén & Sjögren Bokförlag, Stockholm
www.raben.se

Translation copyright © 2002 by Rabén & Sjögren Bokförlag
All rights reserved
Originally published in Sweden by Rabén & Sjögren
under the title *Småflodhästarnas äventyr*
Copyright © 2000 by Lena Landström
Library of Congress Control Number: 2001089557
Printed in Denmark
First American edition, 2002
ISBN 91-29-65500-5

Rabén & Sjögren Bokförlag is part of
P. A. Norstedt & Söner Publishing Group, established in 1823.

Lena Landström

The Little Hippos' Adventure

Translated by Joan Sandin

R&S
BOOKS

Stockholm New York London Adelaide Toronto

On the hippos' fine muddy riverbank, everything
is the same as it always is.

The big hippos are relaxing in the warm water.
The little hippos are splashing and tumbling and paddling
around. And Mrs. Hippopotamus, who lives nearby, is making
seaweed pudding – just as she always does.

But the little hippos wish their diving board were higher.
About as high as Tall Cliff. They are not allowed to go
to Tall Cliff. It's too dangerous.

Every day they ask,
"Can we go to Tall Cliff today?"
But they never get to go.

And then one day, after asking many, many times,
they suddenly get to go.
"We'd better do it right away," they tell each other.

The little hippos have forgotten what was so dangerous in the jungle. Was it snakes?

"Will we be there soon?"
"Maybe we're lost."
"Should we turn around?"

Suddenly, they can see the sky peeking through the trees.
"Tall Cliff!" they all shout at the same time.

What a long way down to the water, the little hippos are thinking.
Luckily, there's a ledge lower down.

But it's a long way to the water from
there, too, they think.
"Okay. Get ready, get set, go . . ."

"Wow!"
"How daring we were!"
"What a splash we made!"
The little hippos are happy, but hungry. They swim upriver
toward home. They completely forget to be careful.

"We can make our diving board higher!"
"And tie a vine to it!"
"And build a slide!"
The little hippos see Mrs. Hippopotamus's bath house.
Soon they'll be home.

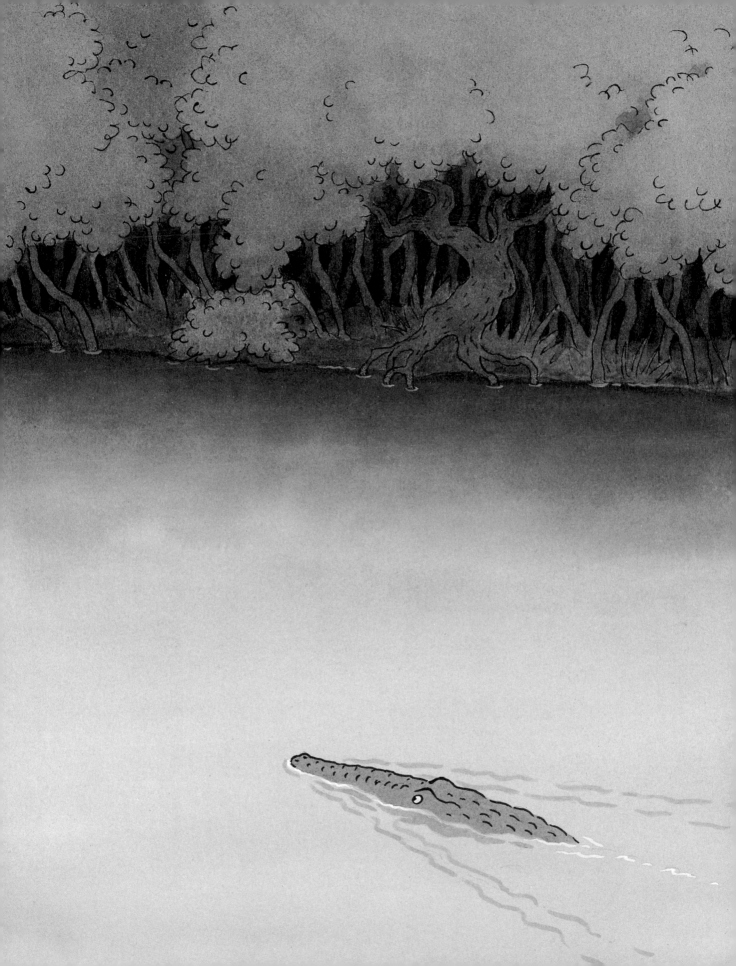

"SCAT!" roars a voice. "GET OUT OF HERE!"

Mrs. Hippopotamus is very angry.
"Don't you dare come around here again!" she yells at the crocodile.
"Next time I'll bite your tail off!"

The little hippos learn how dangerous crocodiles can be.

But they also learn that crocodiles can be funny.

Now the sun has set. It's time for the little hippos to go home. Mrs. Hippopotamus promises to come the next day and help them with their diving board.

Early the next morning, Mrs. Hippopotamus is there
with her toolbox and a stack of boards. The little hippos
come running.
"Can we hammer nails?"
"Can we start with the slide?"
"Can we get the vine now?"
"Give me the saw," says Mrs. Hippopotamus.

By afternoon, it's all finished. Mrs. Hippopotamus packs up her tools. I hope it's not too high, she is thinking.

Down by the riverbank, everything is the same as it always is. The big hippos are relaxing in the warm water. Mrs. Hippopotamus is making her seaweed pudding. And the little hippos are jumping and paddling and sliding and splashing and swinging on the vine. Just as they always do.

"It sure was fun at Tall Cliff!"
"What a big splash we made!"
"It wasn't really all that high, was it?"